Fun China

CHINESE PLACES

Written by **Alice Ma**
Illustrated by **Sheung Wong**
Reviewed by **Judith Malmsbury**

U0111421

Sun Ya Publications (HK) Ltd.
www.sunya.com.hk

Charlie and Ying Ying love dreaming about travelling the world.
As they trace their fingers over China on the map,
a wise and lovely creature from China appears.

Hello, young travellers. I am Dragon C.
I can take you to the beautiful places in China.
Do you want to join me?

Charlie and Ying Ying can't believe their luck.
Both of them eagerly accept the invitation.

3

Can you guess our first stop?
It is the Great Wall of China.
This long wall goes up and down over hills and mountains.
It is like a giant dragon stretching across the land!

The Great Wall of China was built a long, long time ago.
It kept people safe from enemies.
Nowadays, people often say
"He who has not climbed the Great Wall is not a true man."

5

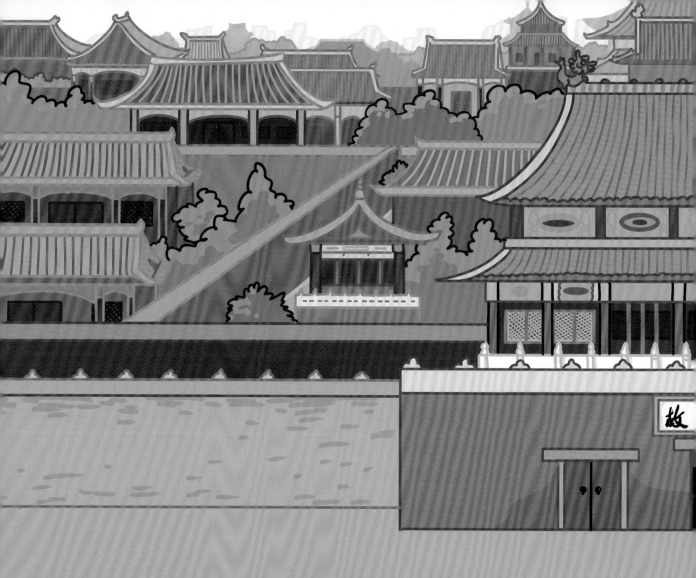

There are many palaces in the world.
One of them is in China — the Forbidden City.
Chinese kings used to live and work there a hundred years ago.

The Forbidden City is very big.
It is about the same size as 100 football fields.
Inside the palace, we can see lots of amazing things.
Come explore how a king and queen lived in the past.

Let's visit the Terracotta Army.
It is an army of life-sized clay soldiers in China.
They were made 2,000 years ago to protect
the first king of China, Qin Shi Huang, after he died.

Take a closer look!
Each soldier has a different face and clothes.
They look like a real army, don't they?
It is one of the most interesting things found from the past!

Would you like to explore more old places?
Let's go to the Mogao Caves in China.
They are a large group of caves,
and there is something really special inside!

Get ready for a hike!
We are going to climb up Huangshan,
a beautiful mountain range in China.

Huangshan, meaning Yellow Mountain,
is famous for its natural beauty.
Many artists and poets have been inspired
by the mountain's views.
It is a magical place
that will take your breath away.
No wonder everyone loves to
explore Huangshan!

Looking for more fresh air?
Jiuzhaigou is a great choice!
It is a national park in China
with colourful lakes, waterfalls and forests.

14

But that's not all!
Many rare animals live there too.
Look! There are a giant panda and a Thorold's deer.
Let's say hello to them.

The giant panda and
Thorold's deer are very rare.
It is lucky to see them!

We should also go to the Classical Gardens of Suzhou.
They are a group of wonderful gardens in China.

These gardens are well-known for
their special designs and lovely plants.
Once you step inside, you will feel calm and peaceful.
It is like being in a fairy tale!
Do you feel the same way?

Another place we must visit is the Fujian Tulou.
They are round buildings in China
made of mud, wood and stone.

A while back, Chinese people lived
in these castle-like places to stay safe and sound.
The Fujian Tulou are very special
and full of history and culture.
They are unlike anything else in the world!

Kids, are you with me? We are going to cross a very special bridge — the Anji Bridge.

Wow, it looks like a moon floating on the water.

Do you know what makes this bridge so special? It is one of the oldest stone arch bridges in the world! It was built more than 1,400 years ago.

Finally, let's end our journey
by visiting the Potala Palace!
It is a grand palace located in Tibet,
which is in the southwest of China.

The Potala Palace is red and white
with many beautiful decorations.
It is very important to Tibetans.
Lots of tourists from all over the world come to see it too!

After the journey,
Charlie and Ying Ying are tired yet happy.

They went to many amazing places in China
that they had only read about in books.
They can't wait to come back and explore more!

English - Chinese Glossary of Chinese Places

The Great Wall of China
TC 萬里長城
SC 万里长城
🔊 Wànlǐ Chángchéng

The Forbidden City
TC 紫禁城
SC 紫禁城
🔊 Zǐjìnchéng

The Terracotta Army
TC 兵馬俑
SC 兵马俑
🔊 Bīngmǎyǒng

The Mogao Caves
TC 莫高窟
SC 莫高窟
🔊 Mògāokū

Huangshan
TC 黃山
SC 黄山
🔊 Huángshān

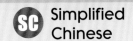

Jiuzhaigou
TC 九寨溝
SC 九寨沟
🔊 Jiǔzhàigōu

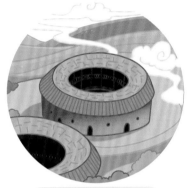

Fujian Tulou
TC 福建土樓
SC 福建土楼
🔊 Fújiàn Tǔlóu

The Classical Gardens of Suzhou
TC 蘇州園林
SC 苏州园林
🔊 Sūzhōu Yuálín

The Anji Bridge
TC 趙州橋
SC 赵州桥
🔊 Zhàozhōuqiáo

The Potala Palace
TC 布達拉宮
SC 布达拉宫
🔊 Bùdálāgōng

Fun China
Chinese Places

Author
Alice Ma

Illustrator
Sheung Wong

Reviewer
Judith Malmsbury

Executive Editor
Tracy Wong

Graphic Designer
Aspen Kwok

Publisher
Sun Ya Publications (HK) Ltd.
18/F, North Point Industrial Building, 499 King's Road, Hong Kong
Tel: (852) 2138 7998   Fax: (852) 2597 4003
Website: https://www.sunya.com.hk
E-mail: marketing@sunya.com.hk

Distributor
SUP Publishing Logistics (HK) Ltd.
16/F, Tsuen Wan Industrial Centre, 220-248 Texaco Road,
Tsuen Wan, N.T., Hong Kong
Tel: (852) 2150 2100   Fax: (852) 2407 3062
E-mail: info@suplogistics.com.hk

Printer
C & C Offset Printing Co., Ltd.
36 Ting Lai Road, Tai Po, N.T., Hong Kong

Edition
First Published in October 2023

All rights reserved.

ISBN: 978-962-08-8270-8
© 2023 Sun Ya Publications (HK) Ltd.
18/F, North Point Industrial Building, 499 King's Road, Hong Kong
Published in Hong Kong SAR, China
Printed in China